P9-CRA-699

what happens next

To Ken Logue, with boundless love — S.H.

For Harper and Edie — C.S.

Text © 2018 Susan Hughes
Illustrations © 2018 Carey Sookocheff

The author acknowledges the following sources for her explanation and understanding of genomes.

DeWeerdt, Sarah E. "What Are Genome Variations?" *What's a Genome?* Genome News Network. 15 Jan. 2003. Online.

"Genomics 101." Génome Québec Inc. 2017. Online.

Owlkids Books acknowledges the financial support of the Canada Council for the Arts, the Ontario Arts Council, the Government of Canada through the Canada Book Fund (CBF) and the Government of Ontario through the Ontario Media Development Corporation's Book Initiative for our publishing activities.

Published in Canada by
Owlkids Books Inc.
10 Lower Spadina Avenue
Toronto, ON M5V 2Z2

Published in the United States by
Owlkids Books Inc.
1700 Fourth Street
Berkeley, CA 94710

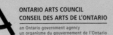
Library and Archives Canada Cataloguing in Publication

Hughes, Susan, 1960-, author
    What happens next / written by Susan Hughes ; illustrated by Carey Sookocheff.

ISBN 978-1-77147-165-7 (hardcover).--978-1-77147-336-1 (softcover)

    I. Sookocheff, Carey, 1972-, illustrator II. Title.

PS8565.U42W43 2018   jC813'.54   C2017-903879-6

Library of Congress Control Number: 2017943555

The illustrations were painted with acryl gouache and assembled digitally in Photoshop.

Design: Danielle Arbour
Edited by: Karen Li and Debbie Rogosin

Manufactured in Dongguan, China, in October 2017, by Toppan Leefung Packaging & Printing (Dongguan) Co., Ltd. Job #BAYDC50

A   B   C   D   E   F

ONTARIO ARTS COUNCIL
CONSEIL DES ARTS DE L'ONTARIO
an Ontario government agency
un organisme du gouvernement de l'Ontario

Canada Council
for the Arts

Conseil des Arts
du Canada

Canada

Owlkids — Publisher of Chirp, chickaDEE and OWL
www.owlkidsbooks.com

Owlkids Books is a division of Bayard CANADA

what happens next

Written by Susan Hughes

Illustrated by Carey Sookocheff

Owlkids Books

**Why I Don't Want to
Go to School Today:**
Bully B.

**What Bully B. Does
at School Today:**
Blocks my way.
Asks me questions that aren't
really questions. Like,
"Why are you so weird?"

What Her Friends Do:
Laugh.

What Everyone Else Does:
Nothing.

**What I Say When Mom Asks How
My Day at School Was:**
Fine.

**What Sparky Does When
He Sees Me:**
Wags his tail. Kisses my face.

What Bully B. Does Today:
Looks me up and down.
Shoves my books.
Calls me Weirdo.

What Her Friends Do:
Laugh.

What Everyone Else Does:
Nothing.

How I Feel Sometimes:
Bad. Really bad.

What I Dreamt About Last Night:
Bully B. chasing me down the hall.
Bully B. teasing me. Bully B. scaring me.

What I Say When Mom Asks Me How I Slept:
Fine.

What I Want to Do on My Way to School:
Hurt something. Squish something.

What I Don't Do on My Way to School:
Hurt something. Squish something.

What Bully B. Does Today:
Swishes past me like I'm invisible.

**What I Say When Mom Asks
How My Day at School Was:**
Fine.

**What Mom Suggests
When She Sees My Face:**
That we could go for a walk,
me and her and Sparky.

What I Do:
Run with Sparky.

Roll down a hill.
Mom does, too.

Hug the Earth. Mom does, too.
Feel the warm grass against my face.
Feel my body sink into the ground.

What Mom and I Do Next:
Lie on our backs, looking up.

What I Say:
Nothing.

What It's Like:
The sky is blue, and big. So big.

What I Feel:
Wow.

What Sparky Does:
Kisses my face.

What I Do Before Bed:
Like always. Look at books.

What Books I Like Best:
One about genomes, which are like instructions for making a person, getting the person going, and keeping that person operating.

One about Earth's waters and rocks, and its tsunamis, volcanoes, and earthquakes.

One about astronomy, which has a foldout map of the universe that shows Earth, other planets, the Sun, and other stars, far, far away.

What I Think About:
That it's good to be alive, a person, here on Earth. But that everything would be better if Bully B. was on another star, far, far away.

What I Say about Bully B. When Mom Comes to Kiss Me Good Night: Everything.

What Mom Says:
That I'm brave for telling her.
That she's sorry I feel scared
and hurt.
That she'll help.

What Mom Says Next:

That everyone has their own way of looking at things and people. That each person's way of looking is made up of where they're standing and how they got there. It's made up of what's in their mind, what's in their heart, and what's in their imagination.

That Bully B.'s way of looking makes me seem weird to her. It only lets her see the ways that I'm different than her.

That the differences Bully B. sees in me, like the way I talk and act, make her feel uncomfortable and maybe afraid. And she doesn't like those feelings.

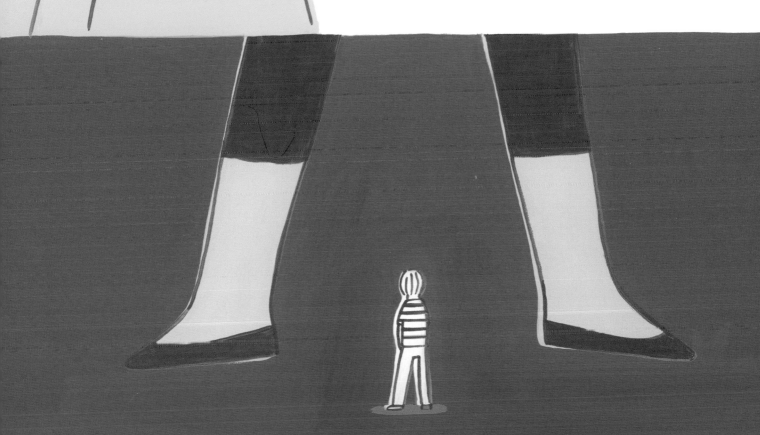

That Bully B. hurts me because it makes her feel in charge of me, and in charge of how she feels about me.

What Happens Next:
Mom says that Bully B. has to change her way of looking. That she needs help to do this. That Mom can go and talk to the principal tomorrow. Or maybe, just maybe, I might want to try to help Bully B. first.

What I Say:
That *Bully B.*'s the one who's mean, and why should I have to help *her*, and it's not fair.

What Mom Says:
That I'm right.

What I Say:
And anyway, how?

What Mom Does:
Says I could tell Bully B. some of the things I love to think about.
That this might help Bully B. change her way of looking.
Then helps me pick three.

What Sparky Does:
Kisses my face.

How I Feel When I See Bully B. the Next Morning: Glad Mom and Sparky are over there, watching.

What I Want to Do When I See Bully B.: Avoid her. Run away.

What I Do Instead: Take a deep breath and say *hey.*

What Happens Next:
I look in Bully B.'s eyes, like Mom
said. I tell Bully B. I need to talk to
her for a minute. Please.

What Bully B. Does:
Frowns. Says I'm such a weirdy
weirdo. Then sees Mom and Sparky.
Shrugs okay.

What I Do Next:

Step back. One, two, three steps.
So I can see Bully B.'s whole body.

What I Tell Bully B.:

That there are seven billion people
on Earth. That every living thing,
and every person, is made up of
genomes. That it's because of
their genomes that each person is
unique, but that we really aren't
so different from each other

That if our genomes were 500-page books, hers and mine would tell the same story and have the same chapters, paragraphs, and sentences in the same order. That the only difference between hers and mine would be that mine might be missing a period on page 279 and hers might have a speling mistake on page 333.

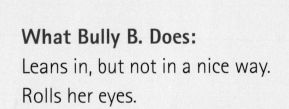

What Bully B. Does:
Leans in, but not in a nice way.
Rolls her eyes.

What She Says, Quietly
So Mom Won't Hear:
You're such a weirdo.

What I Do Next:

Look down.

Tell Bully B. that we're both standing on the surface of the Earth. That about 70 percent of the Earth's surface is covered in water. That about 70 percent of our own bodies are made of water. That without water we would not survive. That Earth has more water than any other rocky planet in the solar system, and so Earth is a perfect place for both of us—for all of us—to live.

What Bully B. Does:
Looks down.
Sees our feet on the ground,
toe to toe.

What She Says, Quietly:
Weird.

What I Do Next:
Look up.
Tell Bully B. that the Earth travels around the Sun, and that once around is about 584 million miles. That Earth travels 67,000 miles per hour. That no matter how far apart we stand from each other on Earth, we're still flying through space together.

What Bully B. Does:
Looks up.
Sways a bit.

What Bully B. Whispers:
W—ow.

What's Different Now:
Not everything. But enough.

What Bully B. Doesn't Call Me Anymore:
Weirdo.

What I Call Her:
Brielle.

What I Still Say When Mom Asks How My Day at School Was:
Fine. But now I usually mean it.

What Sparky Does:
Like always. Wags his tail. Kisses my face.

RADFORD PUBLIC LIBRARY
30 WEST MAIN STREET
RADFORD, VA 24141
540-731-3621